The Travelling Musicians

To Carol,
my children's literature daughter-in-law,
with love

PKP

To Mary Jane

KMD

In slightly different form this adaptation of the Brothers Grimm folktale was written as the narrative for Murray Adaskin's "The Travelling Musicians" commissioned on the initiative of Conductor Paul Freeman by the Victoria Symphony Orchestra and first performed in 1983.

Kids Can Press Ltd acknowledges with appreciation the assistance of the Canada Council and the Ontario Arts Council in the production of this book.

VIKING

Published by the Penguin Group
Penguin Books Ltd, 27 Wrights Lane, London W8 5TZ, England
Penguin Books USA Inc., 375 Hudson Street, New York, New York 10014, USA
Penguin Books Australia Ltd., Ringwood, Victoria, Australia
Penguin Books Canada Ltd, 10 Alcorn Avenue, Toronto, Ontario, Canada M4V 3B2
Penguin Books (NZ) Ltd, 182-190 Wairau Road, Auckland 10, New Zealand

Penguin Books Ltd, Registered Offices: Harmondsworth, Middlesex, England

First published in Canada by Kids Can Press Ltd 1991
First published in Great Britain by Viking 1992
1 3 5 7 9 10 8 6 4 2

Text copyright © P.K.Page, 1991
Illustrations copyright © Kady MacDonald Denton, 1991

The moral right of the author has been asserted

Printed and bound in Hong Kong by Everbest Printing Co. Ltd.

A CIP catalogue record for this book is available from the British Library

ISBN 0-670-84367-9

The Travelling Musicians

Retold *by* P. K. Page

Illustrated by Kady MacDonald Denton

VIKING

IT was one of those beautiful days in summer.
Birds were singing in the leaves.
Wildflowers were blooming in the meadow.
The early morning sun was making diamonds of the dew.
And an old, rather decrepit donkey was munching the sweet grass.
Delicious! Absolutely delicious!
Who wouldn't be happy on such a day?

But the owner of the donkey was not the least bit happy.
He didn't hear the birds.
He didn't even see the sun,
let alone the wildflowers.
Nor could he begin to imagine how good that sweet grass tasted.
All he could see was his donkey.
"Obsolete," he said. "My donkey is obsolete.
Obsolete.
Obsolete.

"Once he carried my grain to market.
Once he pulled my children in a little cart.
Now I have a truck. A big red truck.
And he's obsolete.
Besides which, he's old. And hungry.
All he does is eat."

"Obsolete?" said Donkey, flicking his ears. "That's a word I don't know.
But old. He's calling me old. I understand 'old'.
I'd better make haste before it's too late."
So with all his might he jumped the gate
and galloped away to the highway.

"I shall go to the city," he said.
"I'll make my name!
I'm a musical chap with a musical soul
and I'll play the flute for a living."

He had not gone far before he saw a dog lying on the road –
a despondent looking dog just lying on the road.
"Why, Dog," he said, "you look down in the mouth.
What can be the matter?"

And Dog replied,
"My pedigree is impeccable,
my past performance perfect,
for years I have been a favourite in the house.
And now, just because I am old
and can no longer run when my master goes hunting,
he has threatened to put an end to me.
Why, only this morning he decided to knock me on the head.
Knock me on the head!
I have barely escaped with my life!"

"Cheer up!" said Donkey. "Join company with me.
I'm going to the city to play the flute.
You can play the timpani.
And bark now and then."

And so it came to pass on the highway to the city
that a great, great partnership was formed.
And Donkey and Dog together sang a wonderful, wordless song.

    Hee Haw Hee Haw
    Bow Wow Wow
    Hee Bow Haw Wow
    Haw Wow How

They had not gone far before they saw a cat,
a rag-taggle cat,
crouched by the side of the highway.

"Oh Cat," said Donkey, "you've a hang-dog look – excusing the expression."
"You would have too," cried Cat with a wail,
"if you'd just escaped with your ninth life.
Why, only this morning my mistress tried to drown me!
And simply because I am quite off mice.
I no longer like the taste of them at all.
I much prefer to sit before the fire with a saucer full of milk.
Merely to think of it makes me purr."

"Take heart," replied Donkey, "and you shall have *cream*.
We're travelling musicians,
we need a soprano,
and I'll wager you sing like a bird."

Cat felt so much better after this fine compliment that she began to sing.

> Mee ow Mee ow
> Mee ow ow
> Mee ow mee ow
> Ow Ow Ow

"Bravo!" said Donkey.
"What remarkable luck to meet a cat with so dulcible a voice.
Join us, Cat, and you can play the glockenspiel."

So the three of them, now, set off for the city, there to make their names.

They had not gone far before they came across a rooster
crowing from a gate,
crowing with all his might.

> Doodle doodle doo
> Doodle doodle dee
> Doodle dee doodle
> Deedle doo dee

"Well done!" said Donkey.

"I do declare that you make the most marvellous din.
But it's long past dawn
to judge by the sun,
so what in the world is the matter?"

"Matter!" said Rooster, with an angry flap,
"my mistress plans to give my neck a chop
and put me in a pot
and make me into soup!"

"Nonsense!" said Donkey.
"We can't allow that.
We're off to the city to make names for ourselves.
You've a rousing good voice
and you carry a tune.
Let us form a quartet."

And so they began to sing:

      Hee haw Hee haw
      Bow wow wow
      Mee ow Mee ow
      Doodle Doodle Doo
      Hee Bow Haw Wow
      Mee Doo Arf

Having persuaded Rooster to join them,
they set off once again for the city.

This time, they were in such high spirits,
that they danced as they went,
although Donkey was lame
and Dog had an ache
and Cat had a pain
in the tip of her tail
and Rooster, alack,
had a crick in his neck
and his joints were as stiff
as an iron weather-vane.
Yet they danced till all four
could not dance one step more.

Besides, darkness was falling
and as they were close to a wood
they decided to settle down for the night.

Donkey and Dog lay under a tree,
Cat on a branch overhead,
while Rooster chose, as was his way,
the topmost branch for bed.

They had only just begun to doze –
the night had hours to go –
when from his look-out in the leaves,
Rooster began to crow.

"Time to get up," barked Dog.
"Surely it's not morning yet!" said Donkey.
"I see a light," said Rooster.
"Well, it can't be the sun," said Donkey. "Look again, friend."
"It might be a house," said Rooster.
"Then let's move," urged Dog.
"I've had better beds than these woods
and who knows? There might be bones."
"Or milk," said Cat.

So, once again they set out,
this time in the direction of the light
which grew larger and larger
and brighter and brighter
until they came to a house that was all ablaze with light.

Donkey, being tallest, walked cautiously up to a window
and looked in.
"What do you see?" asked Dog.

"I see a table spread with all kinds of delicious food," said Donkey
in a hoarse whisper.
"And a band of robbers, bold as brass, having
a feast and counting their stolen gold."

"Just the place for us!" barked Dog. "How do we get in?"

So the four musicians came up with a plan.

First, Donkey placed his front feet very,
very carefully against the window.

Then Dog jumped onto Donkey's shoulders.
Cat scrambled onto Dog's back
and finally Rooster flew up and landed
– bop – right on the top of Cat's head.

Then at the arranged
signal, they all
began to sing.

Hee haw Hee haw
Bow wow wow
Mee ow Mee ow

Doodle Doodle Doo

Hee Bow Haw Wow

Mee Doo Arf Baw Wee

How wow Mow Ee Dow

Hee Boo

Bee Mee Doo

Boodle Moo

And, at the same moment, they crashed through the glass,
a great furry, feathery, four-headed monster with hooves and claws.

You should have seen those robbers run!

They were sure, for there wasn't a clear conscience among them,
that some terrible hob-goblin was after them.
One and all, they ran lickety-split to the forest.

But, in the house, what a feast was spread for the lucky musicians.
Such tid-bits and dainties, such mouth-watering bites.
Delicacies beyond anything they had seen on their masters' tables.

They munched and they gobbled and they lapped and they pecked
and when they had swallowed every bite in sight
they turned out the light and settled down for the night.

Donkey lay in the yard on a heap of straw.
Dog stretched out behind the door.
Close to the embers of the fire,
Cat curled up like a ball of fur.
And Rooster, high on the topmost beam,
closed his eyes. Began to dream.

Soon, there was not a sound to be heard.

When the robbers realized that the house was dark
and everything was quiet,
the captain of the band said,
"We were fools to be frightened by a mere noise.
Are we cowards too, to hide all night in the woods?
Robber John, you slip back and find out how things stand."

Shaking a little in his boots as he went,
poor Robber John crept stealthily towards the house.
A twig cracked underfoot and he jumped.
Then . . . total silence.
He couldn't even hear himself breathe.

Reaching the house, he opened the door very carefully.
Apart from the pounding of his heart, he could hear . . . nothing.

Needing a light and mistaking the fiery eyes of Cat for glowing coals,
he blew on them.

Cat spat in his face and dug her claws into his hands.
Dog jumped up and bit him in the leg as he made for the door.
Donkey, wakened from slumber, gave him a well-aimed kick as he passed.
"Cock-a-doodle-doo!" screamed Rooster from his beam overhead.

Poor Robber John, frightened out of his wits,
ran to his friends in the forest,
breathless and nearly fainting.
"There's a terrible witch in the house," he gasped.
"She hissed in my face and scratched me with her long nails.
A murderous villain stabbed me in the leg.
A monster lay in wait in the yard and beat me with a club.
But, worst of all,
on the roof sat the judge, shouting,
'Cock-a doodle-doo-me, bring the robbers *to* me! *To* me! *To* me!' "

And so the robbers, never, but never, returned.

And any day at all, if you happen to pass that house,
whether it be morning, noon or night,
you will hear the musicians making their music for all who care to listen.

Or, for no other reason than the sheer joy of it.

For no other reason than the sheer joy.